This

LOST CREATURES
PICTURE BOOK

was unearthed by,
and is now the
treasured possession of:

Witnesses:

C. G. Salamander

Revered scribe of ancient and modern texts, with huts on the banks of the Adyar and the Lek.

Rajiv Eipe

Hermit palm leaf painter last seen entering the forests north of the Arkavathy.

First published in India by HarperCollins *Publishers* 2025

Building No 10, Tower A, 4th Floor, DLF Cyber City, Phase II,
Gurugram – 122002

2 4 6 8 10 9 7 5 3 1

P-ISBN: 978-93-6569-513-7
E-ISBN: 978-93-6569-758-2

Cover design: Rajiv Eipe

Printed and bound at Nutech Print Services - India

HarperCollinsIn

SONG OF THE ASUNAM

C.G. SALAMANDER
RAJIV EIPE

HCCB
HARPERCOLLINS CHILDREN'S BOOKS

In a sleepy south Indian village where man
and monster lived side-by-side
But mostly kept to themselves,

There lived a boy who was perhaps stranger than the strangest creatures of the wilderness.

When Vetri was eight, he found his grandmother's journal hidden away inside her hut.
It was filled with mythical monstrosities, and notes on how to hunt them.
Vetri was going to be the greatest hunter in the village, even better than his grandmother!

Rompos must be hunted by playing dead and catching them by surprise
Aalais are afraid of the tiniest mice
The Thelen have to be chopped up into a thousand pieces and eaten
Farshi Baharis hate the smell of humans, cover yourself in fish-guts to hunt them

Everyone in the village found Vetri weird.
From the most serious adults
BEASTS DON'T WANDER THIS FAR INTO THE VILLAGE!
To the goofiest children.
PPPTTTTFFFFF
And even his own parents.
WHY IS HE SO SMELLY?

But Vetri didn't care.
He practised his skills every day.
!
YAAAAAAA

One day, on a loud and windy night, when the mist muddled the border between the human and monster sides,
Vetri spotted the scariest, ugliest, most ferocious beast he'd ever seen.
gasp

Its wings, ten times the size of an eagle's
Its body, covered in shimmering scales
Its beak, jagged and mishappen,
And its talons, sharper than the sides of the cliffs where it nested.

The beast swooped
down onto the village
destroying houses
scaring cattle
and sending everyone
into a fear fueled frenzy.
!
But when everyone ran away from the beast,
Vetri jogged towards it.

YOU'RE RUNNING THE WRONG WAY, FOOL!
But Vetri didn't listen.
This is what he'd trained for all his life.

The beast flapped its wings, stretched its talons, and screeched at Vetri.
SCREEECH
But he did not panic.
The boy pulled out his lyre, cracked his knuckles, and played the most beautiful melody.

The Asunam danced and swayed, completely entranced. Then Vetri did as his grandmother's book instructed.
He picked up something heavy, and crashed it as loudly as he could on the ground.
CCRAASSHH
And just like that, the beast collapsed.
THUDD

The entire village was surprised.
Vetri felt like a hero.

Later that evening, when the entire town slept, Vetri was busy reading his grandmother's journal.
YOU WERE JUST CONFUSED, WEREN'T YOU?
SHRIEK
Just as he was about to turn the page—

SHRRIIIEEEEEEEEEEEEEKKKKKKKKKK
The noise was so loud that it woke the entire town.

The Asunam continued shrieking and, by the eighth day, the town had grown sick.
SHRIEEEK
IT SCREAMS ALL NIGHT AND DISTURBS OUR SLEEP!
IT'S GIVING MY CHILDREN BAD DREAMS!
SOMEONE HAS TO DO SOMETHING ABOUT THAT VILE BEAST.

The town got together and voted.
VETRI CAUGHT THE BEAST, SO HE MUST BE THE ONE TO KILL IT!
BESIDES, NO ONE KNOWS AS MUCH ABOUT BEASTS AS VETRI DOES!
YA, AND WE'RE HELPING HIM BECOME A TRUE HUNTER. IT'S WHAT HE WANTS!
GULP

Everyone decided that Vetri would slay the beast and bring sleep back to his town.
SHRIEEEKK

But once inside the cage, he noticed something.
THE CHAINS!

AIYO
The Asunam pounced on Vetri. Grabbing him with its talons, it pinned the boy to the ground. The beast howled and growled. It opened its mouth wide...
SNARL
GROWL
KICK
And licked Vetri.
And that's when Vetri realised that the monster wasn't a monster at all.

Vetri knew he needed to act quickly.
PURRRR
PURRR...
PURR?
He played his lyre to drown out the villagers...
And when the beast was calm, he hopped on and directed it through the backdoor.

Together the two tiptoed through the town.
Vetri noticed that the Asunam was hurting.
I HAVE THE PERFECT PLACE TO HIDE YOU!

Vetri led the Asunam to his grandmother's old hut and tended to it every day.
YOU DON'T HAVE A NAME, DO YOU?
SCHLOP
SHLOOOOOPP
GLOOOP
GLOOP
CRUNCH
THAT'S ALL RIGHT. WE'LL CALL YOU ILANGOVAN.
GULP
GULP

Vetri was happy to finally have a friend, and he could really use one, now that his village had gone back to finding him weird again.
YOU STINK!
But with every visit, Vetri noticed that Ilango was becoming less colourful.
IT SAYS HERE THAT YOU'RE LOSING COLOUR BECAUSE YOU'RE SAD.

Asunams like Ilango lost their colour when they were away from their own for too long.
Asunams needed to walk the song forests, listening to the tune of the woods.
Tends to be loaf-shaped when sleeping
Twitches tail while hunting
Knocks squirrels off trees for no apparent reason
Vetri had finally made up his mind.

He was going to take Ilango back home

across the Great River

beyond the enchanted woods

over the valley of screams

and along the sharpest cliffs.

Thankfully, Ilango could fly.
They would reach the sound
forests in minutes.

Vetri was thrilled
when he saw the
houses on his street
fall beneath his feet.
He stretched his arms to
grab a piece of the cloud,
and stuck out his tongue
to taste the fresh air.

But when they were over the river, the rushing water and
the thundering skies caused Ilango to lose control.

The two spiralled wildly and fell tail first into the water.

Vetri had to act fast. He swam towards the beast and placed his arm around its neck.

gasp.
gasp
SPLASH
Ilango thrashed and splashed, but calmed down when he heard Vetri hum.
SPLASH

Vetri and the Asunam drifted quietly towards the shore.

YOU'RE REALLY AFRAID OF LOUD NOISES, AREN'T YOU?
THE JOURNAL SAYS YOU GET CONFUSED BY THEM. AND THAT A LOUD ENOUGH SOUND CAN KILL YOU!
YOU WERE JUST FRIGHTENED WHEN YOU ATTACKED OUR VILLAGE, WEREN'T YOU?
PPPURRR

Vetri and Ilango took to the skies again, but Ilango struggled to stay in the air. Vetri decided that it was best for them to walk through the forest.
THIS WAY

NO, NOT THERE! THAT BIT IS FILLED WITH MYMEMEX. THEY'LL EAT YOU UP IN SECONDS.
PICASUS LIVE THERE! THEY'LL LURE YOU IN AND THEN ATTACK YOU WHEN YOU'RE LOST.

THAT BIT BELONGS TO THE POOCHANDI TRIBE. THEY'LL SHOW YOU YOUR WORST FEARS.
DON'T EAT THAT! THOSE FLOWERS WILL MAKE YOU LOSE YOUR MIND.
THOSE ARE JUST ROMPO. THEY'RE MOSTLY HARMLESS.

In the valley of lost sounds, Vetri and Ilango heard the shrill cries and the soft wails of lost beasts and children.
The two trudged through the valley, turning a deaf ear to the groans and the sobs.
Whenever Ilango got nervous, Vetri played his lyre.

The two began their climb up the cliff.

There were scary serpents, dangerous dragons, and birds the size of elephants.
But it was a feral Rompo that took Vetri by surprise.
GROWL GROWL
YOU'RE SUPPOSED TO BE PEACEFUL!
GRRRRRR
The Rompo shoved Vetri to the ground and snapped at the air.
GRRRRRR
HELP!

CRACKK
SLAM
But at exactly the right moment, the Asunam stepped in. He grabbed the Rompo and tossed it against the wall.

The hills began to shake. The side of the cliff began to give way. Before they knew it, huge boulders were beginning to rain down on them.
RUMBLE
RUMBLE
RUMBLE
CRUMBLE
RUMBLE
CRASH
CRASH
RUN!

BOOMMM
But the noise was too much for Ilango.
CRASH
CRASH
SSHH
The colours from his scales had all but drained. His wings slumped and his heart slowed.
CRASH
SHSHHHHHH

Vetri tried singing to his friend, but Ilango looked as though he had lost the will to live.

Slowly, he dragged the beast all the way to the forest, and placed him under a tree.

Above, the most melodious songbirds sang.

Vetri tended to Ilango, when all at once he felt a gentle breeze.
flap flap
flap flap flap
He looked up and saw an Asunam flapping its wings.

One by one, more Asunam gathered around their fallen friend. They hummed and they whistled, carrolled, cooed, chirped, cheeped and crooned,

Restoring the colours on Ilango's scales. Colours that the world had forgotten.

Ilango was happier than ever.
Vetri slipped away quietly.

On his way back, on the darkest corner of the cliffs, Vetri encountered a beast that his grandmother's diary hadn't warned him about.
The Iratu were fearless, and lurked in the darkness, patiently waiting for their next meal.
WHAT ARE THEY AFRAID OF?
THINK, VETRI!
But all he could do was tremble in fear as they inched towards him.
Then, he spotted tiny sparks glistening in the sky.

Dozens of Asunam, each brighter and more colourful than the last, flew towards him.
Their scales shone so brightly that it blinded the Iratu and sent them scurrying back into the caves.
They continued to fly over Vetri's head—guiding him, singing for him, and lighting his path home.
And of all the Asunam that appeared that night,

Ilango shone the brightest.

Every year, on the day that Vetri reunited Ilango with its family, the boy made a dangerous trek
Across the river
Along the valley
And over the cliffs
To play his lyre for a friend.
Every year, he would search the skies for a familiar spark.

Brighter than any star in the night sky.

The End

If you liked discovering the Asunam, be sure to search for the next Lost Creature:

COMING SOON!